In memory of Helen Hellman,
librarian extraordinaire! — J. L.

To the books and art that have
always saved my life and made
it more beautiful — E. C.

Scrap Metal Swan

A River Clean-Up Story

written by **Joanne Linden**   illustrated by **Estrellita Caracol**

Barefoot Books
Step inside a story

River clean-up,
Springtime chore.
Townsfolk gather
Near the shore.

Flowing water
Runs downstream.
Save our river:
Make it gleam!

Sunny day,
Silver shimmer.
Old chrome bumper
Meets a swimmer!

River jammed,
No longer free,
All clogged up
With dark debris.

Piles of junk
Along the street.
Friends all help to
Make them neat.

Plastic bottles,
Rusty cans,
Empty milk crates.
Busy hands!

River barge
Picks up junk.
Bang, clang, bump.
Thud, thud, thunk!

Foghorn sounds
Loud and low.
Barge pulls out . . .
Watch it go!

Barge arrives,
Dumps its weight,
Gets paid money
For the freight.

Here come trucks
To haul it out.
See the drivers
Wave and shout!

Tennis ball floats
To the shore.
Artist grabs it,
Looks for more.

Now our friend
Has a plan,
Throws scrap metal
In her van.

Artist's helper
Empties van,
Fills garage,
Turns on fan.

Hammer, anvil,
Chisel, wrench,
Sander, crowbar,
Big workbench.

Blowtorch welds:
Zap, zap, zap!
Form takes shape
From bits of scrap.

Sculptors working
Day and night.
Something's growing,
Tall and bright.

1234
0987

What's that shining
On the lawn?
Artists built
A giant swan!

Now our friends
All join the fun.
Statues gleam
Beneath the sun.

All these artists
Worked together,
Saved the river,
Made some treasure!

River clean,
River wide.
People's pleasure,
City's pride.

River sparkling,
River free.
Ever flowing
To the sea.

Save Our River...

How do rivers get dirty?

People make rivers polluted (dirty) when we aren't careful about where we put our trash or rubbish. Some people throw waste into waterways. People often build factories (places where things like cars and furniture are built) near rivers so they can use river water to help operate their machines. Sometimes when the factories return the water to the river, the water has chemicals or waste from the factory in it. Rainwater can also carry chemicals, like those used for farming and gardening, from the ground into rivers.

Why is polluted water bad?

All living creatures need clean water to live. Polluted water can make humans, animals and plants very sick. All animals eat other animals and plants, so when one type of animal or plant gets sick, it can hurt other creatures too. For instance, if a fish eats plants growing in dirty water, the fish could get sick. Then if a bear eats that fish, the bear could get sick too.

. . . Make It Gleam!

What can we do to help?

At home, we can try not to waste water. One easy way to do this is by turning off the water while you're brushing your teeth! In our communities, we can help with local clean-up projects at parks and waterways. We can also tell our government leaders that clean water is important to us by writing them letters.

The real *Guard Swan*

The author was inspired to write this story by a real statue called *Guard Swan*, created by artist Stephen Bateman in Wisconsin, USA. He built the sculpture after watching trumpeter swans starting their long flight south in early winter. Bateman says, "I thought that they were really brave and I must be brave as well." He built a statue 30 ft (9 m) tall — that's taller than a giraffe!

Bateman used bottles, cans, styrofoam and pieces of metal and wood found in the Mississippi River for his sculpture. He hopes it reminds people to "pay attention to what we're doing when we enjoy our rivers and lakes," showing us how everyday items can end up in the river if we don't pick up our waste: "We will always need a reminder how precious our natural resources are."

Many Kinds of Artists

Visual artists create art we can look at, like the scrap metal swan! Famous visual artists like Leonardo DaVinci, Frida Kahlo, Jean-Michel Basquiat and Yayoi Kusama have created art that changed how people around the world think about things. Art can help us share ideas with one another and make the world a better place. Anyone can create art, including you! Here are some different types of visual artists:

Potters use different kinds of clay to make useful objects like plates, bowls, cups and pots. After shaping wet clay and painting it with glaze, they allow the piece to dry. The dried pieces are then "fired": heated in an oven called a kiln at a very high temperature to harden.

Sculptors use solid materials like clay, wood, resin (a liquid that hardens), wires or stone to create three-dimensional works of art called sculptures or statues. Sculptors may send their work to a place called a foundry to be turned into a metal like bronze. At the foundry, workers use rubber and wax to copy the shape of the sculpture and make it into a mold/mould. Then they pour hot liquid metal into it. When the metal cools, it hardens into the same shape as the original sculpture.

Street artists create art in public spaces. Graffiti artists may use spray paint to create a mural or a portrait on an enormous wall where people can see it. Other street artists might create objects that send a message, such as a swan made out of scrap collected from a river! Shamsia Hassani, Afghanistan's first female graffiti artist, covers the walls of bombed buildings with joyful paintings of women.

Photographers use a camera to take pictures of things they see in the world. They may photograph people, nature, cities or other things that interest them. Many photographers become well known for taking pictures of specific subjects, like Gordon Parks for his images of African Americans.

Painters use brushes and paints to create art on paper, cloth, walls or other flat surfaces. There are several kinds of paint, such as acrylics and oils. There are also a lot of painting "techniques," or ways to use paint. Some artists use paint brushes; others use rollers, sprayers or even splatter the paint! Some paintings look as real as photographs, while others that look like shapes or patterns are called "abstract."

Glassblowers use extreme heat to shape glass into objects. They can make useful glass objects, like drinking glasses, or objects that are decorative, such as hanging ornaments. Vera Lisková was a Czechoslovakian artist whose most detailed piece, *Anthem of Joy in Glass*, uses many delicate spikes of glass to express the harmony of music.

Book illustrators create artwork for picture books, like this one! Illustrators might use paints, pastels, pencils, collage, computers or other materials to make their artwork. Illustrations make picture books interesting for us to look at and also help us understand the words in the book. Some illustrators write their own stories too.

Your Turn to Get Crafty!

Recycling and **composting** help us reduce the amount of waste that goes into landfills and creates pollution. But did you know that recycling actually uses a lot of energy? Trucks and other vehicles carry the materials to recycling plants; these vehicles usually use fuel that causes air pollution. And then recycling plants cause pollution too when they process the recyclables. That's why, in addition to recycling, it's even better to **reduce** how much we use in the first place. We can use less water, paper and electricity. When we need items like clothing or furniture, we can try to buy used things instead of new ones. We can also try to **reuse** the waste we do create.

Here are some craft ideas for reusing materials you might otherwise throw away:

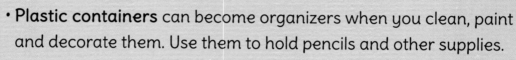

- **Plastic containers** can become organizers when you clean, paint and decorate them. Use them to hold pencils and other supplies.

- **Large cups or glass containers** can be decorated and reused as planters, fairy houses or bird feeders.

- **Paper bags** can become canvases for painting or art activities.

- **Old bits of crayon** can be melted into large crayons or candles, using the oven or the sun.

- **Magazines and newspapers** can be made into paper beads for necklaces or material for collage art.

- **Egg cartons** can become organizers for beads or game pieces, a cute animal craft or seed starters.

- **Cardboard tubes** from toilet paper, paper towels and wrapping paper can be used as music shakers, logs for a pretend campfire, firestarters for a real campfire, a flagpole, buildings for a pretend city or bowling pins for indoor bowling!

T-Shirt Bags

If you have a T-shirt you no longer wear but don't want to give away, you can turn it into a reusable bag! Here are two methods you can try. All you will need is a strong pair of scissors and an adult helper!

One-tie method

1. Lay the T-shirt flat and cut off the sleeves.

2. Cut one of the sleeves open lengthwise. Then cut a long, thick strip of fabric from it.

3. Gather the bottom of the T-shirt and use the strip of fabric to tie the bottom of the t-shirt together. This is the bottom of your bag, so make sure the tie is secure and holds the shirt closed.

4. If the opening around the neck is too small, widen it a bit with scissors, but make sure you leave some of the fabric at the shoulders to use as handles. Pick up the T-shirt by the shoulder loops. Enjoy your reusable bag!

Fringe-tie method

1. Lay the T-shirt flat and cut off the sleeves.

2. Make short vertical cuts about 4 inches (10 cm) long along the bottom edge of the shirt. Cut through both the front and back of the T-shirt at the same time so each strip on the front has a matching one on the back.

3. Tie each pair of strips in a tight knot, making sure no holes are left between knots.

4. When you have a row of knots along the bottom, your bag is complete! If the opening around the neck is too small, see step 4 opposite to widen it.

Author's Note

I was inspired to write this book by a true story. Each spring, volunteers gather along the banks of the Mississippi River near St. Paul, Minnesota, USA, for their annual river clean-up. River junk is collected and piled along the water's edge, where a river barge picks it up and hauls it downstream to be recycled. And every year, artists collect "found objects" from the river junk to use in a sculpture contest. I grew up in northern Minnesota, among pristine woods and sparkling lakes. Each summer, I still return to the woods to recharge my energy. There's a serenity up there that only nature can bring. It's my hope that children everywhere will see from this story how junk can be turned into something wonderful . . . and how we can all take care of the places where we live.

— Joanne Linden

Illustrator's Note

I work entirely in collage, with reused papers that I paint and textures that I create with tools I make myself. For this book I also decided to use clippings of objects from old magazines and encyclopedias. I arrange the cutouts as if they are pieces of a puzzle, glue them together and then take photographs to digitize the illustrations.

I love this story because I identify with the artist characters in it and the message is so related to the essence of my work. I believe you can make art with any materials, which means that art is available to everyone. The same thing happens with these sculptures: each piece brings its own story and magically they transform into something new, like my collages. And if art can also contribute to caring for and cleaning this world that is the only home we have, even better!

— Estrellita Caracol

Barefoot Books would like to thank **Sam Horowitz**, MFA, Sculptor, for his expert input as we developed this book.

Barefoot Books, 23 Bradford Street, 2nd Floor, Concord, MA 01742
Barefoot Books, 29/30 Fitzroy Square, London, W1T 6LQ

Text copyright © 2022 by Joanne Linden. Illustrations copyright © 2022 by Estrellita Caracol. The moral rights of Joanne Linden and Estrellita Caracol have been asserted

First published in the United States of America by Barefoot Books, Inc and in Great Britain by Barefoot Books, Ltd in 2022
All rights reserved

Graphic design by Elizabeth Jayasekera, Barefoot Books
Edited and art directed by Lisa Rosinsky, Barefoot Books
Educational endnotes by Autumn Allen, Barefoot Books
Reproduction by Bright Arts, Hong Kong. Printed in China
This book was typeset in Delius, Cof and Cut-Out

The illustrations were prepared using collages of hand-painted paper and clippings from old magazines and encyclopedias

Hardback ISBN 978-1-64686-498-0
Paperback ISBN 978-1-64686-499-7
E-book ISBN 978-1-64686-579-6

British Cataloguing-in-Publication Data: a catalogue record for this book is available from the British Library

Library of Congress Cataloging-in-Publication Data is available upon request

1 3 5 7 9 8 6 4 2

Barefoot Books
step inside a story

At Barefoot Books, we celebrate art and story that opens the hearts and minds of children from all walks of life, focusing on themes that encourage independence of spirit, enthusiasm for learning and respect for the world's diversity. The welfare of our children is dependent on the welfare of the planet, so we source paper from sustainably managed forests and constantly strive to reduce our environmental impact. Playful, beautiful and created to last a lifetime, our products combine the best of the present with the best of the past to educate our children as the caretakers of tomorrow.

www.barefootbooks.com

Joanne Linden grew up in Kinney, a small town in northern Minnesota, USA, where everyone knew each other and children spent their free time at the small library or playing outside. Joanne loved to read picture books. She still does! Today, she lives in the woods of Eau Claire, Wisconsin, USA, and is the author of many books for children.

When **Estrellita Caracol** was a child, she loved stars, books and cutting out shapes from paper . . . and none of that has changed! She studied graphic design until she realized that what she liked the most was telling stories through her art. Estrellita lives in Buenos Aires, Argentina, with her son and three cuddly cats. She loves to travel and make collages with artists young and old wherever she goes.